THE
TOOTH FAIRY
LEGEND

THE TOOTH FAIRY LEGEND

How The Custom Came To Be

by

Dr. Mac

ILLUSTRATED BY Stephen McAllister

ROUNDTABLE PUBLISHING, Inc.

Malibu, California

Roundtable Publishing Company
29169 Heathercliff Road
Malibu, California 90265

Library of Congress Cataloging-in-Publication Data

McAllister, Francis B.
McAllister, Frances A.
McAllister, Stephen F.

The Tooth Fairy Legend: How The Custom Came To Be

Mac, Dr., 1914–
    The tooth fairy legend / by Dr. Mac: illustrated by Stephen McAllister.
        p. cm.
    Summary: The good Tooth Fairy overcomes an evil spirit and takes all the kingdom's baby teeth to safety in Fairyland.
    ISBN 0–915677–54–7
    [1. Tooth Fairy—Fiction. 2. Fairy tales.] I. McAllister, Stephen, ill. II. Title.
    PZ8.M1703To   1991
    [Fic]—dc20   90–28136
                                                      CIP
                                                       AC

10   9   8   7   6   5   4   3   2   1

Part I

A long time ago, most people believed in evil spirits and feared them. They thought these spirits had magical powers which could harm people. It was also believed that every part of the body was connected by magic.

Parents knew that it was very bad to let their child's lock of hair or baby tooth fall into the hands of an Evil Spirit. If this happened, the spirit could gain a magical power over the child.

The original superstition became even greater among mothers and fathers when some storytellers exaggerated this fear. They warned, "The Evil Spirit can bring a dreaded disease or misfortune to a child through its magical power."

Parents managed the problem of locks of hair. They simply didn't cut hair for keepsakes. But, it is common for baby teeth to become loose and fall out and no one knew what to do with them. Until parents could decide what to do with a baby tooth, the Mother carried it in her apron pocket. It was safe here from the Evil Spirit, who never went near people.

Even when the parents hid the tooth, they always feared it would be found. Other times, the tooth was rolled in salt and thrown into the fireplace. They hoped it would become black and be lost among the ashes.

Part II

One evening, while waiting for supper to cook on the open hearth, a Mother sat down on the long bench at the heavy wooden table. She reached into her apron pocket for the baby tooth, which had been given to her a short time before by one of her children.

"I must do something with this tooth, so the Evil Spirit can't get it," she sighed. While examining it, the little tooth slipped from her fingers and fell to the floor.

"Oh!" she gasped.

She thought it went under the table. But, when she looked, it was not there. It wasn't by the legs of the table or the benches either. While frantically searching for the tooth, she saw a mouse scamper along the floor near the wall on the far side of the room.

It was not uncommon to see a mouse in the house in those days, so the sight of a mouse did not disturb her.

But, soon the mouse reappeared from behind the hearth. The Mother saw the baby tooth at the very same time. The tooth had slid across the floor toward the hearth. She moved quickly from behind the table to get it.

But the mouse was quicker. It grabbed the tooth in its mouth, ran to a wide crack in the kitchen wall and disappeared.

The Mother could not believe what had happened. Now there was no way she could ever find the tooth.

"What will I do?" she wondered and began to cry.

When the Mother went to bed that night, she was so worried that she could not sleep.

The next morning, she told her neighbors what had happened. They, of course, knew about the Evil Spirit and what occurred when it got possession of a baby tooth. Many wept in pity for the Mother and her child.

But, one neighbor had an idea.

"Go to the Queen," she said. "Tell her your sad story. Surely she can offer some advice. The Queen is known to have a great interest in the welfare of her people."

So, the Mother decided to make the trip to the castle. It was a far distance away, atop the highest mountain peak. Since there was no time to lose, the Mother left at once.

It took many, many hours to arrive at the castle. A guard greeted her and listened sympathetically to her story. It reminded him of when his son and daughter were children and his worry about their baby teeth. The guard immediately led the Mother to the Queen, who received her graciously.

The King and Queen were aware of the problem regarding baby teeth. They worried not only about their own young Prince and Princess, but for all the children in the Kingdom.

After the Queen had heard the story of how the mouse stole the tooth, however, she clapped her hands in delight.

"Oh," she exclaimed excitedly. "Now we have a solution for the baby tooth problem!"

But the Queen realized her words had upset the Mother.

"I know mice like to carry things to their nests," she quickly explained, "but I didn't realize a mouse would pick up a baby tooth. There is not a safer place to hide a baby tooth than in a mouse's nest. The Evil Spirit would never go near one."

"Oh," the Queen exclaimed again. "This is good news! The King and all our people will be very, very happy."

With that, the Mother left the castle and returned home.

The next day, the Mother told her neighbors, "I'm happy, and so is the Queen, because the tooth is in a safe place. Messengers will announce the King's proclamation to all the people."

And so they did:

Hear ye! Hear ye!
Place your children's baby
teeth where mice can find them.
The mice will carry them to their
nests. The teeth will be safe there.
The Evil Spirit does not like mice
and will not go near them.

The King's message became known everywhere, even in Fairyland. The fairies were not happy about letting a mouse have a baby tooth. However, it was much better than worrying about the Evil Spirit. One fairy thought, "There has to be a better way."

Part III

One day, a Good Fairy left her home in Fairyland and went to a nearby village to watch the children play. She loved children very much and spent a great deal of time being near them.

While the Good Fairy enjoyed the merriment of the children, she overheard two Mothers. One was telling the story about how a mouse took a baby tooth into its nest to keep it from falling into the clutches of the Evil Spirit. This reminder prodded the Good Fairy into action. She decided to find another way of keeping baby teeth out of the hands of the Evil Spirit. She disliked the Evil Spirit for all the sadness it caused the land. But the idea of letting a mouse take a child's tooth into its nest also saddened her.

After much thought, she had an idea for a happy solution. "I'll pick up the baby teeth! I'll pick them up and bring them to Fairyland!" She said this over and over, and, the more she repeated it, the more she liked the idea.

She knew she would need help to make the plan work, so she decided to go to the Queen. The Good Fairy asked her friends in Fairyland, "If the Queen accepts my plan, will you help me store the baby teeth in their proper places under each child's name?"

"Yes," her friends replied. They were overjoyed with the idea of bringing the baby teeth to Fairyland. "We will build a Baby Tooth Museum right in the heart of Fairyland."

The Good Fairy knew the teeth would be safe there. They could never fall into the hands of the Evil Spirit or be carried away by mice. And the Good Fairy knew that she would have keepsakes from all of her children friends—keepsakes that would last forever.

After much thought and planning, the Good Fairy went to the castle to talk with the Queen. She told the Queen about the conversation she had heard between the two Mothers.

Then, she said, "I would like to change the way baby teeth are now kept safe. I agree that everything possible should be done to keep the Evil Spirit from having a baby tooth, but I don't like the idea of mice carrying baby teeth into their nests."

The Queen nodded.

"Have you a better plan?"

"Yes," smiled the Good Fairy, "I have a better plan. I will gather up all the baby teeth and take them to Fairyland. My friends in Fairyland will help. They have offered to build a Baby Tooth Museum. It will be the perfect place to keep the baby teeth of every child from the world over."

"This is a splendid idea and one that makes very good sense," admitted the Queen. She knew it was impossible for any living thing to enter Fairyland without the consent of a fairy.

"But, there is one more thing we must consider," the Queen added.

"The word must be spread throughout the land, so there can be no misunderstanding about this new way to dispose of baby teeth. Now, we must inform the King. He will order his trusted messengers to inform all the Town Criers, who will, in turn, tell all Mothers and Fathers. Then, every parent can pass this custom on to their children. This way of disposing of baby teeth will be carried over from one generation to another, and will continue to be known forever and ever."

The Queen and Good Fairy went to the King and told him about the plan.

The King was delighted with the idea of a Baby Tooth Museum in Fairyland. Without hesitation, he offered the services of his trusted messengers to announce the new plan throughout the Kingdom.

"I, too, have always disliked the practice of letting a mouse have a baby tooth," he said. "But, until now, there seemed to be no other way. I wish you could begin picking up baby teeth immediately!"

"I do, too," the Good Fairy agreed. "Don't you think the parents will be glad to give them to me instead of mice?"

After a brief pause, the King answered softly, "I'm not so sure that they will. People are in the habit of giving teeth to mice. It's not easy to change people's habits."

The King sat quietly for a few moments. Finally, he spoke. "I believe I know a way. I will donate a large sum of money to the Fairyland Bank. The money can be used for gifts. Each time you take a baby tooth, you leave a coin in its place," he said.

The Good Fairy listened, amazed. "That's wonderful! Now I'm sure every parent will give me the baby teeth instead of letting mice have them."

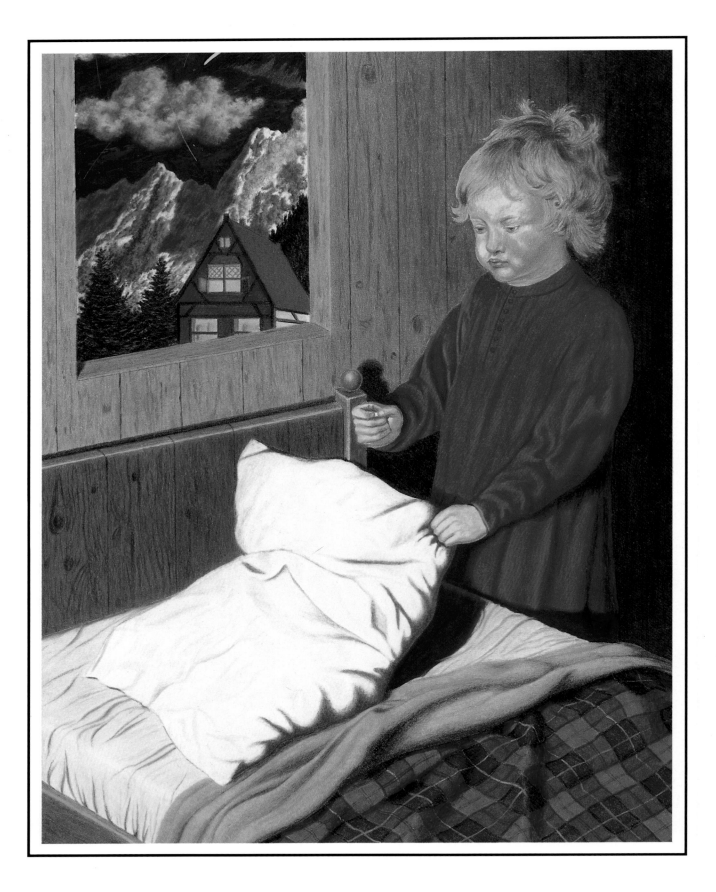

"I believe they will, too," the King agreed. Then, he asked, "Where should the baby tooth be left, so you can find it?"

"That question will require some thought," the Good Fairy answered.

The King and Queen agreed that this was a problem they would all have to consider for a while.

The three realized that the Evil Spirit could easily get the tooth if it were left in plain sight. So, after considering many hiding places, it was decided that under a child's pillow would be just right. The tooth would be placed there at bedtime. Then, the Good Fairy would come during the night and know exactly where to find it.

When all the details were complete, the King called his trusted messengers and told them the whole story.

In turn, they were to tell all Town Criers. At the same time, arrangements were made to move the King's monetary gift to the Fairyland Bank.

The Good Fairy thanked the King and Queen with all her heart. Then, she hurried back to Fairyland, for there was much work to be done. First, she helped her friends build the Baby Tooth Museum.

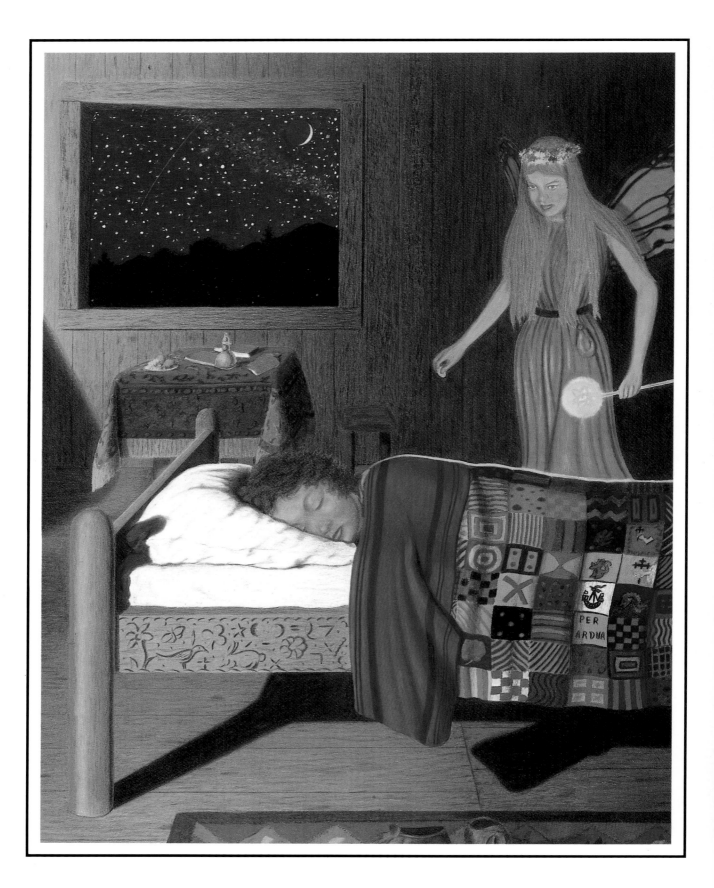

It was now time to begin collecting the baby teeth. Each night, the Good Fairy visited every home where a baby tooth had been left for her. And never once did she forget to leave a coin in its place.

Many years passed.

One day, the King said, "I have decided to honor the Good Fairy for the work she has done so long and so faithfully. Not only for the children of our kingdom, but for the children of all lands."

He summoned his Court. After much discussion, it was suggested to set aside a special *Good Fairy Day.*

"The Good Fairy is remembered every day by someone," the King stated. "Therefore," he continued, "I proclaim that the Good Fairy will have a special title."

The Court agreed that the King's idea was the best way in which to honor the Good Fairy.

Hence, the following decree was issued by the King:

Hear ye! Hear ye!
From this day forward
for all time, the Good
Fairy shall have a special
title all her own. The Good
Fairy is to be called
"The Tooth Fairy."

And it came to pass. To this day the order stands. She is called "The Tooth Fairy" by everyone.

Although the Evil Spirit is no longer feared, children place each baby tooth under their pillow. The Tooth Fairy always comes during the night and takes it back to the Baby Tooth Museum. And, of course, she always leaves a coin in its place.

The Tooth Fairy knows—and so do children everywhere—that baby teeth are safe in the Baby Tooth Museum, where they will last forever.

A LITTLE MORE HISTORY

For a long period of time the rodent played an important role in disposing of baby teeth.

In warm climates rodents often lived in thatched roofs. Here parents developed a little ceremony for disposing of baby teeth. The child would stand with his or her back toward the hut and toss the tooth overhead to the roof. A rodent would find it and carry it away to its nest.

In Central Europe and other places with a cool climate, the baby tooth was placed where a mouse would find it. This was in the house or barn where mice were. Sometimes the tooth was dropped into a hole where a mouse had a nest.

The belief was that "the Evil Spirit" did not like rodents and never went near them or where they lived.

In Africa, the father, early in the morning, would take a baby tooth and throw it into the sun, hoping that nothing could see it and that it would never be found.